MOLLY'S LIES

The Seabury Press,
815 Second Avenue, New York, New York 10017

Copyright © 1979 by Kay Sproat Chorao
All rights reserved. No part of this book may be reproduced
or transmitted in any form or by any means, electronic or
mechanical, including photocopying, recording or by any
information storage and retrieval system, without
permission in writing from the publisher.
Printed in the United States of America

LIBRARY OF CONGRESS CATALOGING IN PUBLICATION DATA

Chorao, Kay.   Molly's Lies.
"A Clarion book."
SUMMARY: Challenged by a classmate on the first day of
school, Molly stops making up stories and admits her fears.
[1. Honesty—Fiction. 2. Fear—Fiction] I. Title.
PZ7.C4463Ml   [E]   78-12383
ISBN 0-8164-3225-2

MOLLY'S LIES

story and pictures by
KAY CHORAO

A CLARION BOOK
The Seabury Press • New York

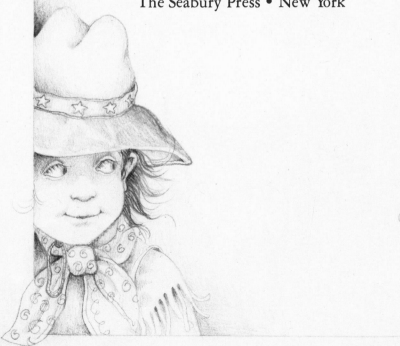

Today was Molly's first day of school.

She frowned at the new clothes her mother had set out for her.

"Hurry and get dressed, dear," called her mother from the kitchen.

Molly stuffed her new red jumper and her new striped shirt and her new red shoes in a waste basket.

"I can't. My clothes got lost," yelled Molly.

Molly could hear her mother's wood-bottomed shoes clomp-clomping down the hall. Toward her room.

Quickly Molly dressed in her favorite clothes.

"MOLLY," said her mother at the door. "Take off that Prairie Rose costume this minute."

"They called from school. They said I could stay home and play cowgirl," said Molly.

"I'm in no mood for your tales, young lady."

A corner of red jumper stuck out of the waste basket. Molly's mother saw it.

"And get dressed as fast as you can in these," she said.

"I *hate* that red jumper and I don't want to go to school," grumbled Molly.

But slowly Molly put on her school clothes and walked to the kitchen.

"Please eat your breakfast quickly or we'll be late," said Molly's mother.

A pile of granola cereal sat in Molly's bowl. It looked like a mountain to her. If she were Prairie Rose she could lasso it.

"I can't eat," said Molly, slipping off her chair. "What if the teacher asks me to spell something or do arithmetic? I don't know how."

"Don't be frightened. No one expects you to know those things yet," her mother told her.

She kissed Molly's forehead and together they walked to the door.

Molly squeezed her mother's hand and they got on the elevator.

The elevator slowed down.

A new boy from apartment 7A got on with his mother.

Molly frowned at him, and he frowned back.

"Why does that girl have those things on her thumbs?" the boy asked.

"Shhhhhh," said his mother, smiling at Molly.

Molly slid behind her mother.

When the elevator stopped they all got off and walked in the same direction.

"Are you going to P.S. 57 too?" asked the boy's mother.

"Yes," said Molly, frowning.

"Is that fat girl going to *my* school?" asked the boy.

"Shhhhh," said his mother.

"I'M NOT GOING," cried Molly.

But they all went inside P.S. 57.

When the mothers went home, Molly found herself in a room with children she didn't know, and toys in tidy lines, and a teacher who was too busy to notice her.

"What are those things on your thumbs?" asked the boy from 7A.

"A crocodile bit me," said Molly.

The boy sat on the floor next to Molly. He stared at her thumbs.

"He lives in my closet and I feed him chocolate raisins."

"Can I see him?" the boy asked.

"He bites. You better not try to see him. But I can. I'm Prairie Rose and I'm brave."

"You're not brave," said the boy. "You're fat and you lie."

Then he ran away.

Molly wanted to cry, but she was afraid the other children would laugh. Instead she went to the paint room and put on a big plastic apron.

Molly had never painted before in her life.

"Are you a good painter?" asked a red-haired girl.

"Of course," said Molly.

"A *very* good painter?" asked another girl.

Molly dipped her brush in the red paint, and then in the blue paint.

"I'm a very, very good painter," said Molly, dipping her brush into the yellow paint.

The paints were turning a strange color.

"Here's a beautiful flower," said Molly.

She raised her brush to the paper. It was heavy with paint, and made a huge puddle of dirty brown that dribbled down the paper and dripped all over the floor.

"She lied," giggled the two girls. "She can't paint."

"I know," said the boy from 7A, peeking around the easel.

Molly ran to her cubby. She hid her face and cried.

The teacher came over and took her hand. He led her to the crayon table.

Molly would show them how smart she was. She would write her name.

Slowly she printed her name, the way her mother had shown her. She sat back and admired her letters M O L L Y.

"What a pretty bird," said the teacher.

"It's not a bird. It's my name."

The teacher pinned Molly's name on the bulletin board.

"That's a dumb bird," said the red-haired girl.

"It's my *name*," said Molly.

"Don't believe her," said the boy from 7A.

Molly chewed her thumb bandage, and wished she could go home and never come back.

After juice and cookie time some of the bigger boys started a game called Fireman. They slid down a rope from the platform over the doll corner. To make it scary one boy made the rope swing back and forth.

"Come on up," they called to the boy from 7A.

The boy from 7A looked at the tall platform and the rope swinging wildly past the doll house.

Molly could see he was afraid to play Fireman.

"Go on up," said Molly, joining the others.

"I don't want to," he said.

"Go on," Molly teased.

Maybe he will crash and it will serve him right, Molly thought.

"Skeerty. Skeerty-cat," the boys and Molly chanted.

Molly looked at the boy. His eyes were wet and he was biting his lip. Molly could see he was going to cry.

"Yellow skeerty cat," the others chanted again.

Suddenly the boy seemed so much smaller than all the rest. And there was no one to defend him.

"He's not *so* scared," said Molly in a small voice.

The boy stepped closer to Molly.

"The day our building caught on fire he slid on a rope all the way to the street," said Molly in a louder voice.

"Did you really?" asked a boy.

"Um-hummmm," said the boy from 7A.

"The super said he was a very good rope slider," Molly added in an even louder voice.

The boys looked doubtful, but the teacher stopped the game and they ran away to listen to the teacher play his guitar.

Molly sat on the doll house.

"What's your name?" asked the boy from 7A.

"Molly."

"I'm Joseph."

"Were you scared to go up there?"

"Yes," said Joseph.

Molly looked at him. "Why did you say that? Weren't you afraid I would laugh at you?"

"If I lied you would know I was lying," Joseph said. *"Then* you would laugh."

Molly looked at her thumbs for a long time and thought. Then she looked at Joseph again. "Know what?"

"What," said Joseph.

"My Mom wraps my thumbs because . . . because. . . ." Molly put her head down. He would laugh. "I won't tell."

"Tell," said Joseph.

"Because I suck my thumbs," whispered Molly.

Joseph didn't laugh.

"Sometimes I lie, too," he said. "You're not really fat."

On the way home from school Molly skipped next to her mother.

"You know what? Joseph said I lied because I said a crocodile bit me."

"Joseph was right," said Molly's mother.

"And you know what else? Everyone laughed at me because I said I was a good painter, then I made a terrible painting that dripped all over the floor."

"Everyone makes messes sometimes," said Molly's mother.

"And you know what else?" said Molly. "I wrote my name and everyone said it looked like a bird, and when I said it was my name no one believed me."

"Oh?" said Molly's mother.

"Uh humm, because I USED to tell soooo many lies," said Molly.

Then she skipped ahead to walk with her new friend Joseph.